ana

ANDREW

Planting Peanuts

by Christine Platt
illustrated by Anuki López

Calico Kid
An Imprint of Magic Wagon
abdobooks.com

About the Author

Christine A. Platt is an author and scholar of African and African-American history. A beloved storyteller of the African diaspora, Christine enjoys writing historical fiction and non-fiction for people of all ages. You can learn more about her and her work at christineaplatt.com.

For every child, parent, caregiver and educator.
Thank you for reading Ana & Andrew! —CP

To my brother and sister and our crazy and happy days at home. —AL

abdobooks.com

Printed in the United States of America, North Mankato, Minnesota.
102020
012021

THIS BOOK CONTAINS RECYCLED MATERIALS

Written by Christine Platt
Illustrated by Anuki López
Edited by Tyler Gieseke
Art Directed by Candice Keimig

Library of Congress Control Number: 2020941643

Publisher's Cataloging-in-Publication Data

Names: Platt, Christine, author. | López, Anuki, illustrator.
Title: Planting peanuts / by Christine Platt ; illustrated by Anuki López.
Description: Minneapolis, Minnesota : Magic Wagon, 2021. | Series: Ana & Andrew
Summary: Mama and Papa bring home supplies to start a backyard garden, and Ana & Andrew go along to the local nursery to pick up peanut seedlings. They plant the seedlings and harvest the peanuts, and their parents teach them about one of the first African American botanists.
Identifiers: ISBN 9781532139703 (lib. bdg.) | ISBN 9781644945247 (pbk.) | ISBN 9781532139987 (ebook) | ISBN 9781098230128 (Read-to-Me ebook)
Subjects: LCSH: African American families--Juvenile fiction. | Gardening--Juvenile fiction. | Plants—Juvenile fiction. | Peanuts--Juvenile fiction. | Botanists--Juvenile fiction. | Carver, George Washington, 1864?-1943—Juvenile fiction.
Classification: DDC [E]--dc23

Table of Contents

BIO
Fertilizer

Chapter #1
The Garden

One Saturday morning, Mama walked in the front door carrying a very large bag. "Honey, can you please get the rest of the bags out of the car?"

Papa went to the car and brought in two more large bags.

"What's all this stuff?" Ana asked.

"Yeah," Andrew wanted to know. "Are there toys inside?"

Ana giggled. "Yes, me and Sissy would like to know if there are toys inside too."

"I definitely did not buy three bags of toys." Mama laughed. "But, why don't you unpack the bag that I brought in and see for yourself?"

Ana and Andrew reached inside. Andrew pulled out a pair of scissors, some gloves, and two small hand rakes.

"Andrew, look at this tiny shovel!" Ana pulled a shiny shovel out of the bag. It had a violet handle.

"That's called a trowel," Mama explained.

Ana and Andrew looked at each other, confused. "Why do we need a trowel?"

"Because we're planting a garden!" Mama said enthusiastically. "The other two bags contain planting soil."

"Oh boy!" Andrew did a wiggle dance.

"Hooray!" Ana hugged Sissy. "I've always wanted a garden just like Grandma and Grandpa have in Savannah."

"Because we live in the city, our garden won't be as big as your grandparents'," Papa said. "But we have enough space in our backyard to plant just what we need."

"Think of one special item you'd both like to grow," Mama encouraged. "We're going to buy our seeds tomorrow."

Ana and Andrew were very excited. They couldn't wait to get started.

Chapter 2

Seeds and Seedlings

The next morning Papa announced, "It's time to go to the nursery to get seeds for our garden!"

"Nursery?" Ana asked. "Isn't that for babies?" Aaron, her baby brother, giggled as she tickled his chin.

Mama laughed. "*Nursery* is also another name for a gardening center."

"Well, do they have baby plants there?" Andrew asked.

Mama laughed again. "Yes, I suppose they do. Seeds and seedlings are like baby plants."

They left for the nursery soon after.

At the nursery, Ana and Andrew couldn't believe how many plants were growing inside. Some were in small pots and others in large containers. Some even hung from the ceiling. It was like a mini jungle!

A store clerk greeted them.
"Welcome to District Nursery. I'm
Mr. Thomas. How can I help you?"

"We are starting our first garden,"
Mama explained. "Ana and Andrew
are going to plant something special."

"Yes!" Ana giggled and hugged Sissy. "We're going to grow our favorite treat!"

"Me and my sister are going to plant peanuts," Andrew said excitedly.

"Great choice!" Mr. Thomas said. "It's spring, so that's the perfect season to plant peanuts. You'll harvest them in late summer."

"What's *harvest*?" Ana asked.

seedlings

"That's when you'll be able to pick and eat them!" Mr. Thomas smiled. "I'll be right back."

Soon he returned with two small potted plants. "These are peanut seedlings."

"Baby plants." Andrew smiled.

"That's right," Mr. Thomas said. "Plant them in your garden and water them every day. Soon you'll see yellow flowers growing. And on the first day of September, dig up the peanuts that grew underground."

After selecting everything they needed, Mama and Papa paid for their items at the register. On the way home, Ana and Andrew carefully held their seedlings. They couldn't believe they were going to grow their own peanuts!

Chapter #3
Mr. Carver

Starting the garden was fun! Papa used wood to create a raised gardening bed.

Then, everyone put on their gardening gloves and helped fill the bed with planting soil—a special dirt used to grow fruits and vegetables. Afterward, they used the hand rakes and trowel to dig holes for the seeds and seedlings.

"Andrew, you sure look like a young George Washington Carver over there!" Mama said happily.

"Who's that?" Andrew asked as he carefully placed his peanut seedling in the small hole.

"He was a botanist, a special type of scientist who studies plants," Mama explained. "In fact, Mr. Carver was one of the first African American botanists."

"Wow!" Ana carefully placed her peanut seedling in another hole and filled it in with soil.

"He lived during the 1800s," Papa added. "He worked at Tuskegee University, an all-black college in Alabama."

"I bet you'll never guess what Mr. Carver used to help cotton farmers," Mama said.

"What?" Ana asked.

"Peanuts!" Mama exclaimed.

"How?" Andrew wanted to know. "Can peanuts help cotton grow?"

"Yes, how?" Ana asked. "Because you can eat peanuts. But you can't eat cotton."

"Yes, Andrew," Papa said. "Peanuts *can* help cotton grow. And you're right too, Ana. Let's finish planting all the seeds and seedlings in the garden. Then I'll tell you more about Mr. Carver and his important work."

After all their seeds and seedlings were planted, everyone covered the holes with planting soil.

Mama made labels for each item, and they placed the labels in the dirt. Finally, they were finished.

"Look at our first garden," Mama said proudly, and everyone smiled.

Then, Ana and Andrew went inside to clean up and eat lunch. They couldn't wait to learn more about Mr. Carver.

Andrew's Peanuts

Mama & Papa's tomatoes

Ana's Peanuts

Chapter #4
Harvest Time

When they were finished eating lunch, Papa said, "Now, let me tell you about Mr. Carver and boll weevils."

"Boll weevils?" Ana giggled. "That sounds funny."

"I suppose it is a funny name for an insect," Papa mused. "But cotton farmers don't think boll weevils are funny at all. They love to eat cotton crops."

"But guess what boll weevils don't like," Mama said. "Peanuts!"

"Silly boll weevils!" Andrew exclaimed. "Don't they know peanuts taste better than cotton?"

Papa laughed. "Well, boll weevils don't think so. Mr. Carver told farmers to plant peanuts with their cotton crops to keep boll weevils away.

"He also invented products like peanut butter so farmers could earn money from the peanuts they planted."

Ana and Andrew wanted to be good botanists like Mr. Carver. They helped Mama and Papa water the plants every day. Soon, yellow flowers grew atop the peanut seedlings.

"Look!" Ana said excitedly. "Our peanuts are growing!"

Ana and Andrew continued taking good care of their seedlings. They marked off each day on the calendar. Finally, it was the first day of September.

"Today's the day!" Andrew did a wiggle dance.

"Harvest!" Ana hugged Sissy.

Mama and Papa helped them dig in the dirt. Soon, they saw dozens of brown nuts.

"Peanuts!" Ana and Andrew exclaimed.

After carefully cleaning their harvest inside, Mama put the peanuts in a large bowl. Everyone took turns eating handfuls of the tasty nuts.

"Do you think Mr. Carver would be proud of us?" Ana and Andrew asked Papa.

"Yes, he would." Papa smiled. "He'd be proud indeed."